Printed by CreateSpace, an Amazon.com company
Available from Amazon.com, CreateSpace.com, and other retail stores
Also available on Kindle
ISBN-13: 978-1491275924
ISBN-10: 1491275928
Library of Congress Card Catalog Number: 2013915491
www.babybuzzybee.com

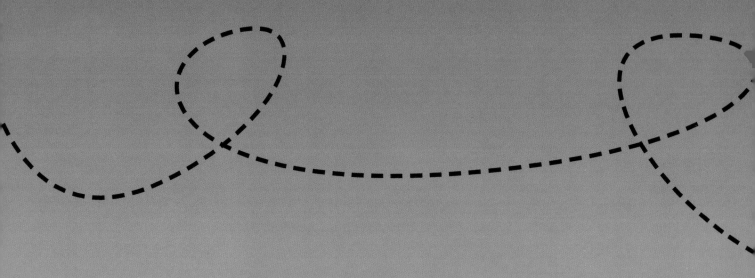

For my son Oliver — who has kindled my imagination,
and helped me to play like a child again.

Baby Buzzy Bee plays hide and seek

written by Robert C. Randolph

illustrated by Joelyn D. Brickner

Daddy Buzzy Bee, will you play hide and seek with me?
I will, Baby Buzzy Bee. Let's buzz to a tree.

Baby Buzzy Bee, where are you hiding from me?
Are you hiding in this green tree? No.

Are you hiding in these yellow trees? No.

I am hiding in this pink tree!

You are a good hider, Baby Buzzy Bee.
Let's buzz to another tree!

Baby Buzzy Bee, where are you hiding from me?
Are you hiding in this fall tree? No.

Are you hiding in this snowy tree? No.

I am hiding in this Christmas tree!

You are a good hider, Baby Buzzy Bee.
Let's buzz to another tree!

Baby Buzzy Bee, where are you hiding from me?
Are you hiding in this lemon tree? No.

Are you hiding in this apple tree? No.

I am hiding in this pear tree!

You are a good hider, Baby Buzzy Bee.
Let's buzz to another tree!

Baby Buzzy Bee, where are you hiding from me?
Are you hiding in this monkey's tree? No.

Are you hiding in this koala's tree? No.

I am hiding in this owl's tree!

You are a good hider, Baby Buzzy Bee.
Let's buzz to another tree!

Baby Buzzy Bee, where are you hiding from me?
Are you hiding in this Joshua tree? No.

Are you hiding in this pine tree? No.

Are you hiding in this oak tree?
Yes!

I found you Baby Buzzy Bee.
I found you in the oak tree!

You found me Daddy Buzzy Bee.
You are so good at finding me.

That is because I love you Baby Buzzy Bee and I will always find you even if you are not hiding in a tree.

Robert C. Randolph grew up playing in the mountain town of Lake Tahoe. He met his wife at the University of California at Berkeley and followed her to San Diego where he completed writing classes at the University of San Diego Adult School. Robert and his wife have been married since 2006, welcomed their son Oliver in 2009, and their daughter Evelyn in 2013. The family enjoys playing outside in San Diego's parks, beaches, and zoo.

Joelyn D. Brickner is a graphic artist, copywriter and illustrator based in Southern California. She is a graduate of San Diego State University, where she earned a bachelor of arts degree in graphic design with an emphasis in fine art. Her graphic design work has appeared in The San Diego Union-Tribune and for companies including Asset Marketing Systems.

Made in the USA
San Bernardino, CA
25 November 2013